Song
of the
Wild Violets

by Peggy Thompson

The Book Publishing Company
Summertown, Tennessee

Once upon a time not so long ago, there lived a little girl. Her name was Maggie. Maggie was nine years old. She lived on the edge of a large Indian reservation. Maggie and her parents were Chippewa.

2

Life on the reservation was very hard. Maggie's father could not find a job. There were no jobs open to the Indian people. The land on the reservation was not good to farm because it was swampy.

Father told Maggie many stories about living on the
reservation when he was a boy back in the 1940s.

"Many of the people lived in tar paper shacks," he said. "There was no heat or running water. The four of us kids slept in one big old bed. There was only one blanket to keep us warm in the winter." Father shivered at the memory.

Maggie cuddled closer to him.

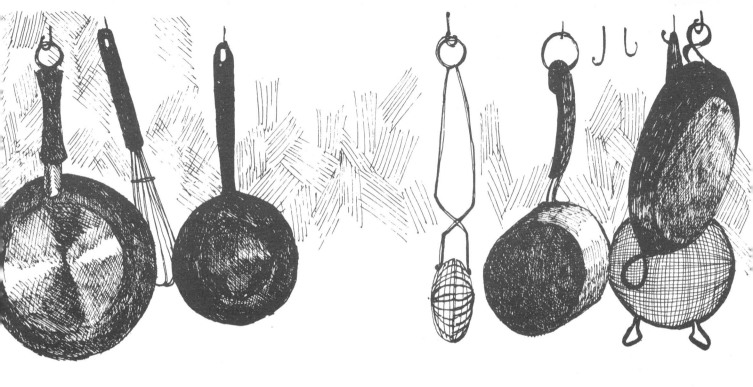

"Sometimes we didn't have enough to eat," Father continued. "Then we had to walk to Grandma Pool's house up the road. She always had a big pot of soup on the stove. She fed us bowls of the best soup in the world and big plates of fry bread."

Father was silent as he sat lost in his thoughts.

Suddenly he smiled and chuckled to himself.

"What are you thinking, Daddy?" asked Maggie.

"Well, honey, it is a fact that your Great-Grandpa cooked, too. He made the hottest chili in the neighborhood. He was a very wise man and greatly respected by all the folks around, whether they were red or white. In fact, white people would come all the way out to the reservation from town just to talk with him. When they came, Great-Grandpa fed them large bowls of steaming red hot chili until they coughed and spluttered and the tears ran down their cheeks! After they were gone Great-Grandpa would laugh and laugh."

Maggie was puzzled. "Why did he laugh, Father?"

"Laughing was better medicine for your Great-Grandpa than hatred, honey," Father answered. "The white people were very cruel to our people. The pain had to come out somehow."

Maggie was silent as she remembered that Great-Grandpa's father had been one of the few members of the Cree tribe to walk the famous march called "The Trail of Tears." He had watched most of his people die of abuse and starvation at the hands of the white soldiers.

Then Maggie understood.

Times had changed from the days of Father's stories. Now the government built tract houses for the Indian people to live in. Maggie and her parents lived in a tract house. It was very square and poorly made. Maggie hated it.

Father told her a story once about a relative who had lived in a tar paper shack all his life. When the government built a tract house for him he could not feel comfortable in it. He could not understand the reason why. Then he realized, "There is no tar paper smell!"

He covered the entire house with tar paper. Then the relative felt at home.

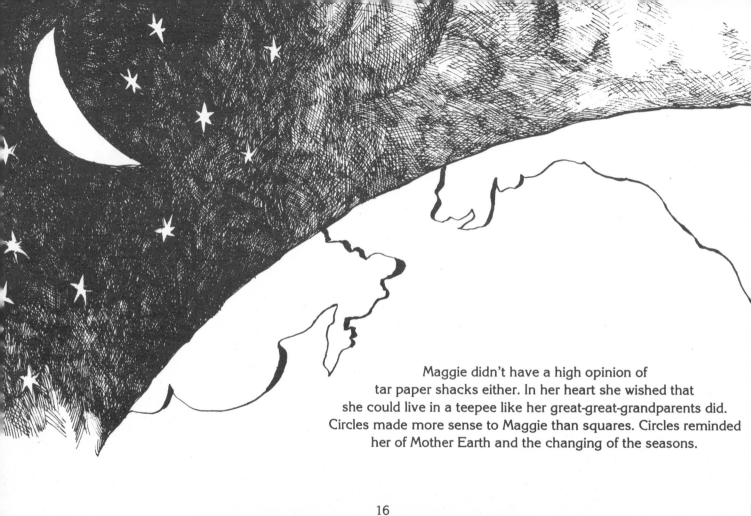

Maggie didn't have a high opinion of
tar paper shacks either. In her heart she wished that
she could live in a teepee like her great-great-grandparents did.
Circles made more sense to Maggie than squares. Circles reminded
her of Mother Earth and the changing of the seasons.

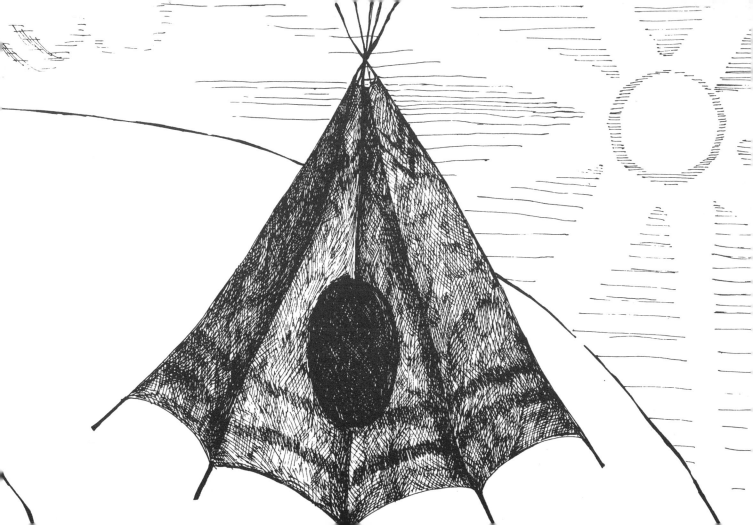

Because of her feelings towards the tract house, Maggie preferred to spend much of her time outside. In back of the house there was a large forest. It was made up of pine, maple, cedar, and oak trees. Squirrels, moles, possums, chipmunks, and many birds lived there. They were Maggie's closest friends. Every day she went to visit them with scraps of food. The animals ate from her hands.

Maggie respected the animals as equals. She knew how to be still until the little animals trusted her. She grew to understand their language and gestures. Eventually Maggie began to talk to them. They were good listeners, too. Mr. Squirrel and Mrs. Chipmunk tilted their heads to one side as they heard the day's stories of her life in the tract house.

Over time Maggie learned much from the little animals who were her friends.

They taught her the art of listening well. They taught her to be so still that she could hear the sound of leaves growing. They taught her how to have fun as they played games with each other until Maggie laughed with delight.

Above all, they loved her.

Maggie learned how to trust and love them in return. Maggie's intuition grew and grew. Mother Nature was her teacher, her nurturer, her friend.

One day Maggie decided that she would honor the forest and her animal friends. She would draw them.

She took paper and pencil outside and sat down by her favorite tree. Mr. Squirrel sat on a limb nearby and chattered to her in curiosity.

Maggie laughed.

She looked around slowly and saw a bunch of wild violets growing in the grass. Maggie began to draw them. Soon she was lost in the delight of creating.

Hours went by as she tried to draw the beauty in front of her.

As she saw deeper and deeper into the miracle of life before her, Maggie began to feel a deep and peaceful joy which she had never experienced before. All of a sudden, time stopped.

Peace flooded through her. Her body felt like it was gently weighted down by a loving presence that made her cry. It was so big, so overpowering, gentle yet deeper than words could ever describe.

Maggie heard music. It was the harmony of the universe pulsing through her and through all living things.

The music lifted her up into a wide vision of a sacred and great love that surrounded her like white wings. As Maggie became more and more connected with the music, she knew in her heart that this great love was stronger than any poverty or racism in the world. Maggie sank deeper and deeper into the music until she *was* the music. All of a sudden, she knew that this is where she belonged.

Maggie had come home. She stayed there for some time, filled with a joy that made her ache.

Slowly the music stopped and she became aware that Mr. Squirrel was chattering to her for a handout. Maggie reached into her pocket and gave him a handful of sunflower seeds.

She went into the house to help her mother fix dinner.

"Maggie, why are you smiling?" asked Mother.

"Because I feel free!" answered Maggie. "Today I drew, Mother, and I felt so happy that my heart aches!"

Mother said nothing, but in her heart she was glad. She knew that Maggie was beginning to discover something big that would give her life meaning for the rest of her days.

Maggie went to sleep that night, her eyes resting on the stars outside her window.

"For some reason, they are shining very brightly tonight," Maggie said to herself. She began to pray.

"Great Spirit, You have made the stars so beautiful. They are shining for me right now. You made the violets that I drew today. You have made me and Mother and Father. You have made so much that is good. Why is it, Great Spirit, that with all the beauty you make, we have to live in this ugly house? Why do my parents have to live without hope because they have no money to leave this place? Why is it that my people have suffered so horribly? It's not fair." Maggie sobbed as tears ran down her cheeks.

The stars were silent, but they glowed brighter than ever. Maggie fell asleep.

That night Maggie had a big dream. In the dream Maggie was sitting in a circle with her parents and some of her tribe. Everyone was telling stories. There was venison, wild rice and mushrooms, fry bread, and good hobo coffee to drink. In the midst of the laughing and talking, Maggie stood up and slowly moved to the center of the circle. Everyone was silent as they watched her gather energy to speak.

"Last night I had a dream," Maggie began. "A great white bird came to me and planted sacred seeds inside me. Soon, flowers of creativity grew inside me: wild violets. I painted them and the paintings breathed life." She paused and her voice became weighted with her spirit.

"The dream showed me that the great white bird has brought the sacred seeds to each one of us," she continued. "This future time will be a time when wild violets grow among our people. We will cover our lives in beauty, making and breathing new life into everything around us."

Maggie had spoken. She sat down next to her parents.

The circle of people sat in silence and took in the power of her vision. As they let the meaning of her words sink into them, a great wave of warmth, like sunshine, rose up within each person's soul.

The dream faded and Maggie slept peacefully until morning.

When Maggie woke up, the sun was shining in her window. Her eyes slowly gazed around the golden room. On her dresser she saw a brown paper bag with a red ribbon tying it closed. A small index card was attached to the ribbon. Maggie jumped up and ran to the package. It was a present all right! And it wasn't even her birthday! She opened the card.

"Maggie, dearest, this present is for you to make your dreams come true. Love, Mother."

Maggie tore open the bag and found a beautiful set of watercolors, two paintbrushes, two drawing pencils, and a small sketchpad. She jumped up and down in excitement and ran downstairs.

Mother was in the kitchen having her morning cup of coffee.

"Mother! Thank you so much for such a wonderful gift! You have read my heart!" Maggie told her mother about the dream she had the night before.

Mother was impressed. Together they made a prayer of gratitude to the Great Spirit for the gifts of the dream and creativity.

Soon Maggie went outside to draw with her new art supplies. Mother sat at the kitchen table and thought a long while about Maggie's dreams.

"Once I was creative, too," she thought. "Somehow, life dragged it out of me with so much worry and work. I have been too busy to relax. That is a bad example for my Maggie. I wonder where that old star quilt I was working on went to."

Mother went to find her quilt. She found it in the back of the bedroom closet. As she spread the quilt out, she was swept away by the beauty of the rainbow colors. She had begun making it for her husband to take to the sweat lodge years ago. Mother took the quilt back into the kitchen and poured another cup of coffee. Under her breath she said, "The chores can wait until later." And Mother began to quilt again. As she quilted, a song rose in her heart and she began to sing a song of joy.

Outside, Maggie heard her mother singing. Maggie smiled to herself as she recognized her mother's song. It was the same song that Maggie had heard while she was drawing the wild violets.

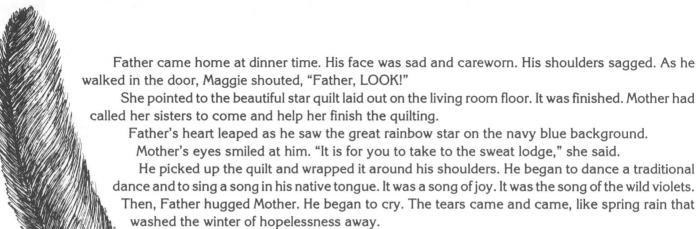

Father came home at dinner time. His face was sad and careworn. His shoulders sagged. As he walked in the door, Maggie shouted, "Father, LOOK!"

She pointed to the beautiful star quilt laid out on the living room floor. It was finished. Mother had called her sisters to come and help her finish the quilting.

Father's heart leaped as he saw the great rainbow star on the navy blue background.

Mother's eyes smiled at him. "It is for you to take to the sweat lodge," she said.

He picked up the quilt and wrapped it around his shoulders. He began to dance a traditional dance and to sing a song in his native tongue. It was a song of joy. It was the song of the wild violets. Then, Father hugged Mother. He began to cry. The tears came and came, like spring rain that washed the winter of hopelessness away.

Soon after, Father went to the sweat lodge. He was cleansed deeply.

The Great Spirit showed him that he was to return to his traditional ways. He was to let go of the abuse from the white people. He was to let go of many of their teachings.

Eventually, Father became a teacher to both red and white people about Indian ways. He was respected for his wisdom. Eventually, teaching became the way in which Father earned his living.

Mother continued to make beautiful quilts. She gave them away as gifts of love.

Maggie grew up to become an artist and a musician. She wrote her own lyrics and music. Her main theme song grew out of the song she had heard when she was nine years old and drew the wild violets.

34

Dedication
to Callie, Min, Matt and Doug

The stories of life on the reservation are from my husband's childhood.
The dream and vision are from my childhood.

Special thanks to Annie Plumley-Thompson for modelling for the drawings of Maggie. Thank you also to Sara and Jessie Plumley Thompson, Liz and Maggie Thompson, Edith and Pete Peterson and my husband, Bob, for further modelling. Bob also drew the cover and title page of this book.

Library of Congress Cataloging-in-Publication Data
Thompson, Peggy, 1952-
    Song of the wild violet / Peggy Thompson
        p. cm.
    Summary: A young Chippewa girl and her parents are unhappy with life on the reservation, until she helps the family return to traditional Indian ways.
    ISBN 0-913990-37-X: $5.95
    1. Ojibwa Indians—Juvenile fiction. [1. Ojibwa Indians—Fiction.   2. Indians of North America—Fiction.] I. Title.
PZ7.T371983So 1993
[Fic]—dc20   93-641
                                  CIP
                                  AC

    0 9 8 7 6 5 4 3 2 1

NATIVE AMERICAN BOOKS FROM

THE BOOK PUBLISHING COMPANY

PO Box 99
Summertown, TN 38483
or call: 1-800-695-2241

Basic Call to Consciousness	$ 7.95
Blackfoot Craftworker's Book	$11.95
Children of the Circle	$ 9.95
Dream Feather	$11.95
Good Medicine Collection:	$ 9.95
Life in Harmony with Nature	
How Can One Sell the Air? NEW EDITION	$ 6.95
Indian Tribes of the Northern Rockies	$ 9.95
Legends Told by the Old People	$ 5.95
A Natural Education	$ 5.95
The People: Native American Thoughts and Feelings	$ 5.95
The Powwow 1993 Calendar	$ 6.95
Sacred Song of the Hermit Thrush	$ 5.95
Song of the Seven Herbs	$10.95
Song of the Wild Violets	$ 5.95
Spirit of the White Bison	$ 5.95
Teachings of Nature	$ 8.95
Traditional Dress	$ 5.95